The *Way*

of the

Cross

D1374310

The *Way* of the *Cross*

by
Roy and Revel Hession

Original Title:
The Calvary Road
Adapted into Simplified English
by
J.W. McMillan

CLC ❖ PUBLICATIONS
Fort Washington, Pennsylvania 19034

Published by CLC Publications

U.S.A.
P.O. Box 1449, Fort Washington, PA 19034

GREAT BRITAIN
51 The Dean, Alresford, Hants. SO24 9BJ

AUSTRALIA
P.O. Box 419M, Manunda, QLD 4879

NEW ZEALAND
10 MacArthur Street, Feilding

ISBN 0-87508-238-6

© Evangelical Literature Service, Madras, India
Adapted from *The Calvary Road* by Roy Hession
© 1950 Christian Literature Crusade, London
*This American edition 1973 under special arrangements with
the Indian and British publishers.
Not for sale in Asia, Africa and the West Indies.*

This printing 2001

Old Testament quotations are from *The Living Bible*, © 1971 by Tyndale House Publishers, Wheaton, IL. Used by permission. Unless otherwise indicated, New Testament quotations are from *Good News for Modern Man, The New Testament in Today's English Version*, © American Bible Society 1966, 1971. Used by permission of the American Bible Society, New York, and Wm. Collins & Co. Ltd., London. Other New Testament quotations are from *The Living Bible*, © 1971 by Tyndale House Publishers, Wheaton, IL. Used by permission.

ALL RIGHTS RESERVED

Printed in the United States of America

_____ACKNOWLEDGMENTS

We are grateful to the following for their help in producing this Everyday English Edition of *The Calvary Road*:

The author, Mr. Roy Hession, for his gracious permission to adapt the book in this way.

Mrs. Ida David and Mrs. Rona Locke, for kindly going through the manuscript and making many helpful suggestions for improvement.

The Ruanda Mission, for their kind permission to use the drawing Not *"I," But Christ*, on page 20.

J. W. McMillan

_____CONTENTS

INTRODUCTION

THE MESSAGE of this book is of great importance to all Christians everywhere in these days. I am sure, from my own experience, as well as the things I have seen in our mission in the last three years, that it is a vital word from God Himself. For a long time I thought of revival as being an experience which people longed to have, but which came only very rarely as the Holy Spirit was suddenly poured out on a group of people. But at the same time I felt there was something which I did not know. Then I found out that revival was continuing in a certain mission field. It was not a sudden or passing thing, but was continuing. From this I was sure that they knew some secret which we needed to learn. Then I was able to have heart-to-heart fellowship with them. First, one of our own missionary leaders visited the field and his life and service were completely changed. When some of their missionaries were on furlough, we were able to have conferences with them. Finally, two of their national brethren lived for six months at our headquarters.

From these people I learned and saw that revival begins in a person and can be experienced at once. It is the day-by-day experience of any Christian who lives in the light. But I saw that living in the light means a completely new feeling towards sin. It means that we call sins by their real name—*sins*. We do not pass over pride, hardness, doubt, fear, self-pity and the like as being just human weaknesses. No, we recognize that they are sins. We have to be willing to be broken, and to confess these things at the feet of the One who was broken for us. His blood does not make us clean while we make excuses, but it does cleanse us from sin when we are ready to confess sin as sin. Revival is the daily experience of the soul which the Lord Jesus has filled till it is running over with the Water of Life.

We, as a company of witnesses for Christ, are also beginning to learn another lesson. The rivers of life to the world do not flow out in their fullness through one man, but through the body, the team. We must not only be broken and open in our upward relationship with God, but also with one another. Teamwork in the Holy Spirit is one of the keys to revival. We must learn and practice the laws of a living fellowship. We are just beginning to experience this in our own mission.

I do not need to say any more. Roy Hession and his wife explain the whole matter in this little book. But we have seen God at work in our midst. In six of our workers, some of them leaders, there has been a complete spiritual change. The little streams of blessing in their own lives have been coming together to make a bigger stream. At times, as a company, we have had the experience of the early Christians:

"When they finished praying, the place where they were meeting was shaken. They were all filled with the Holy Spirit" (Acts 4:31). Here and there, where our workers are fighting against sin and Satan, we have news of showers of blessing. We believe that God is preparing many of His people to serve Him in a special way these days. We believe that what God is saying to us through this revival, which this book explains to us, is a word from the Lord for us for our day. May God use it greatly to bring revival— in our lives, in our fellowships, and in our churches.

Norman P. Grubb
Hon. Secy. Worldwide Evangelization Crusade
London

PREFACE

IN APRIL 1947, I organized an Easter Conference. I invited several missionaries to come as speakers. I chose these men because they had been experiencing revival for some years in the area where they lived. I wanted to know more about revival. What they told us, however, was very different from what I had expected them to say. I had thought of revival as a great work of God among unsaved people. I thought it occurred when, in large and noisy meetings, many people came to trust in Christ. But these men showed us something very simple and quiet. They told us their own experiences of revival.

As these men gave their testimonies, I saw that I myself had a great need. I realized, as I had never done before, that I needed to be revived! But I came to know this very slowly. As I was one of the speakers at the conference, I was more concerned about the needs of others than about my own need. But my wife and many others who were at the conference saw their need. They humbled themselves before God. They experienced in a new way the cleansing power of the blood of Jesus.

I myself did not experience it. I was surprised to think that the way was so simple. I knew what I had to do, but that was all. The conference came to an end. Many testified to the way the Lord Jesus had broken them. Their hearts were filled to overflowing with the Holy Spirit. I, however, was not able to say that this had happened to me. I was still trying to fit the things I had heard into my own ideas of what the Bible taught about this. But afterwards I stopped trying to do this. I came humbly to the Cross. I confessed my own sins. It was like a new beginning in my Christian life.

When Elisha told Naaman to dip himself in the River Jordan, Naaman became proud. He did not want to do the simple thing which the prophet had commanded. I was like that. But when Naaman did as the prophet had told him, he was made clean. His skin became like that of a little child. Something like this happened to me. A new chapter began in my life. But ever since then I have had to choose, day by day, to die to myself. I have had to come at all times to the Lord Jesus, to make Him my all, and to receive cleansing by His precious blood. This is the reason why it is a new chapter in my life.

At this time, my wife and I were publishing a little magazine called *Challenge*. By means of this magazine, we were trying to help young Christians to get to know the Lord Jesus in a deeper way. In the next number of this magazine, we naturally wrote about the truths which God had shown to us. We printed the message of revival as it had come to us. Because it contained this message, more and more people wanted to read the magazine. In later numbers of

Challenge we wrote more about the message of revival. Still more people wanted to get the magazine.
We were very surprised. Almost every day we got
letters from people who told us how God was blessing this message. They wanted still more copies of
the magazine. Some of these letters came from coun-
tries far away. The magazine was reaching them.
Many of God's people read it and began to be revived in their own lives. People translated the message into French and German. We could see that God
was using us to bring this message to others in a way
we had never expected.

We knew that we were not worthy to be used in
this way. We had nothing to be proud about. The
articles in *Challenge* had been written because we had
known revival blessing. They were the *effect* of the
revival and not its *cause*. God was working in the
hearts of many people in different parts of the world.
When those who had been revived told others what
had happened to them, their friends became hungry
for the same kind of blessing. They too came to the
Cross and were revived. In this way blessing spread
from one person to another.

Because of this the magazine became better
known. In it we tried to use simple language from
the Bible to tell of the blessings which so many were
beginning to enjoy. This little book is simply a col-
lection of some of the articles which we put in *Challenge*. At present we cannot send out any more copies of this magazine. But people are still writing to
ask for copies of the numbers which contained these

articles.

It is plain that still more people want to know the message of revival. God's people have a growing thirst for the Rivers of Living Water. We have been encouraged by God's blessing on the previous work we have done so we have put together in book form the more helpful articles from *Challenge*. We have added two more chapters. Now we are sending them out, asking God to use them as He thinks best.

We cannot say that the whole subject is set out here in an orderly way. Each chapter was written as an article for *Challenge*. It was intended to be complete in itself. Now these articles are put together in one book. Some subjects are mentioned in more than one article. Some truths are repeated again and again. So do not regard this as an ordinary book, to be read through once. It would be best to read each chapter on its own.

Do not think that this book is just our own work. We have learned the truths in it with other people in different places. They, like ourselves, have begun in a new way to walk the Way of the Cross. Any one of them might have written these chapters. Our fellowship with others who have learned these truths is continually growing. More and more people are being quietly helped and blessed by the movement of revival. This shows how important these matters are.

Now what do we mean by revival? Many people will be surprised as they read about revival as explained in these pages. People usually think of revival as a great religious awakening when many unsaved people realize that they are sinners and turn to Christ. There is often much excitement. Some people think that these happenings of God's Spirit are not meant to be understood. They say we can only pray that God will work in this way and wait until He begins to do it. At the same time many Christians believe that they cannot know victory over sin in their lives. But people think that the Church must somehow witness about Christ even when many Christians do not themselves show forth new life.

However, many of us are finding that revival is not at all like this. It need not be a showy outward thing at all. The person who is seeing his sinful condition in the light of the Cross will certainly not want to make a show of it. The outward, public part of revival is the least important part. Missionaries who have experienced revival often say very little about this part of it. Instead, they want us to understand clearly what God is saying to *us* about *ourselves.*

Revival is not something which God does to unsaved people. It is His work among His own people. They have life, but sometimes it grows weak. Revival is the strengthening and reawakening of that life. The unsaved person needs life, because he does not have it. But the Christian who has wandered away from God needs to be revived. The more fully and openly we confess our sins to God, the more fully He will revive us. When this happens among Christians, God will work among the unsaved in new power. We shall see Him working in grace in their hearts.

Evan Roberts was a great preacher in the Welsh

Revival. He used to say, "Bend the Church and save the people." When God's people are humbly walking with Him, unsaved people will turn to God. The two things go together. The world has lost its faith because the Church has lost its zeal.

We must say one last thing. The reader must read these pages in the right way. He must have a real hunger in his heart. He must be dissatisfied with the state of Christians generally. Most important of all, he must be dissatisfied with himself. He must be willing for God to work in himself first. He must not expect Him to begin with someone else. He must know and believe that God can and will meet his need. It is only in this way that God will be able to bless him through reading this book.

If the reader is a Christian leader, he must give very great attention to these matters. He must be willing first to admit his own need. He must seek God's blessing with all his heart. If he does this, God will not only bless the leader himself, but also those whom he serves. He must be the first to humble himself at the Cross. If he wants his people to be willing to see the true nature of their sin, he must be ready to see the true nature of his own sin. Think of what happened in Nineveh after Jonah preached. The king himself arose from his throne and covered himself with sackcloth. He sat in ashes to show that he was truly sorry for his sins. When he did this, his people did the same.

But, if you are *not* a leader, do not look at your leaders. Do not wait for them to act. God wants to begin with each one of us. He wants to begin with you.

May God bless you all.

Roy Hession

Chapter 1

_____ BROKENNESS

W E WANT to show, very simply, what revival is. Revival is just the life of the Lord
Jesus poured into human hearts. The Lord Jesus is
always the Victorious One. The angels in heaven are
always praising Him because He has won the victory. We may know failure and lack of fruit: He is
never defeated. There is no limit to His power. But
how can we share in His power? How can His power
be shown in our hearts and lives? How can we serve
the Lord in *His* power? We must be in a right relationship with Him. If we are, He will fill us with His
victorious life. That life will then overflow from us
to others. This is the real meaning of revival.

How can we get into a right relationship with
Him? The first step is this: our wills must be broken.
We must do His will, not ours. To have a broken
will is the beginning of revival. It is a painful thing.
It makes us humble. But it is the only way. We must
know what it means to say, "Not I, but Christ" (Galatians 2:20). First of all, our proud self must be broken. Only then can the Lord Jesus, who lives in us,

fully reign in our hearts. Only then can He truly show Himself through us. Our own self must give up its rights. Our self is hard. It does not want to obey God. It likes to show that it is in the right. It wants to go its own way. It wants to claim all its rights. It always seeks glory for itself. The self must bow to God's will. It must confess that it is wrong. It must give up its own way. It must obey the Lord Jesus. It must give up all its glory. Only in this way can the Lord Jesus have all and be all in our lives. We must die to self.

We must honestly look at our lives. We shall see that there is much of self in us. We often try to live the Christian life in our strength. (The very fact that we talk about *trying* to live the Christian life shows that "self" is still reigning!) Self tries to do Christian work. Self easily gets annoyed. Self becomes envious of others. It resents others. It finds fault. It gets worried. It is hard. It is not willing to give in to others. It is shy. That is why we must be broken. God cannot do a great work in the lives of those who are ruled by self. He wants to fill us with the fruit of the Spirit (Galatians 5:22–23). But this is just the opposite of self! Until our selfish spirit has been broken and crucified, the fruit of the Holy Spirit cannot be seen in our lives.

How can we be broken? This work is both God's work and ours. God shows us that we need to be broken, but we must choose. We must be willing for God to show us the truth about ourselves. Unless we do this, we cannot have fellowship with Him. We must be ready to listen to what God says to us. If we are ready to do this, He will show us the things which come from our proud, hard self. These are the things which cause God pain. When He does this, we can do one of two things. We can become proud and refuse to repent, or we can humbly bow our heads and say, "Yes, Lord." The man who knows, day by day, the meaning of brokenness is the man who humbly agrees to what God shows him about himself. This is something we need to do every moment of our lives. We must daily be broken before God. This may cost us a great deal. We shall have to give up our rights. We shall no longer live to please self. Sometimes we may have to give back something we have wrongly taken from others.

There is only one place where we can be really broken. That place is the cross of the Lord Jesus. He was willing to be broken for us. When we realize this we must be willing to be broken for Him. He always had the very nature of God but He did not think that by force He should try to become equal with God. Instead, of His own free will He gave it all up, and took the nature of a servant (Philippians 2:6–7). He was God's servant—and man's servant as well. He was willing to have no rights of His own. He had no home of His own. He had no possessions of His own. When He was cursed He did not answer back with a curse (1 Peter 2:23). He was willing to let men tread on Him. He did not strike back or defend Himself. He went humbly to the cross. There He was broken for us. He became man's sin-bearer. He carried our sins in His body to the cross (1 Peter 2:24).

In some of the Psalms, David foretold the coming of Christ. In one verse in the Psalms we read these sad words: "I am a worm, and no man" (Psalm 22:6). There is a great difference between a snake and a worm. When a man hits a snake, it rears up. It hisses angrily. It tries to hit back. The snake is a real picture of self. But a worm does not do this. It does not try to hit back. It will allow you to kick it or crush it under your foot. The worm is a picture of real brokenness. This is what Jesus was willing to become for us: a worm and no man. Why did He do this? He knew that we were like worms. We had sinned against God. We had no right to come to God. All we deserved was hell. He now calls us to be like worms for Him. He wants us to be in the place that He was in on earth. We see this in the Sermon on the Mount. The Lord Jesus there taught His disciples not to take revenge on someone who does wrong to them (Matthew 5:39). He told them to love their enemies

(Matthew 5:43). He told them to give and expect nothing back (Luke 6:35). These things are only possible if self is broken. And this is only possible as we look at the vision of the Love which was willing to be broken for us on the cross.

> Lord, bend that proud and stiffnecked "I,"
>   Help me to bow the head and die,
> Looking to Him on Calvary,
>   Who bowed His head and died for me.

This is not something which happens only once in our lives. There will be the first time when God shows us these things and we die to self. But from then on we must always be dying to self. Only in this way can the Lord Jesus be always showing His life through us (2 Corinthians 4:10). Each hour of the day we must choose to obey God. This choice will be made hundreds of times each day. We will have no plans or time of our own. Our money will belong to God, to use as He wants us to use it. We shall have to do day by day what He wants us to do. And as we submit to God, we shall have to submit to those round about us. Only in this way will we show that we are really submitting to God. People will make us sad. They will annoy us. They will make us angry. God will use these things to break us. In this way He will make us even deeper channels for the Life of Christ to flow out to others.

There is only one kind of life that pleases God. There is only one kind of life which really knows victory. That is God's life. Our life can never bring victory. We may try very hard to win, but we cannot. Our life has self at its center. It is the enemy of God's life. We can never be filled with God's life until we let Him put our life to death every day. And each day of our lives we must choose to let Him do that!

Chapter 2

_____CUPS RUNNING OVER

W E BEGIN to be revived when our wills are broken. But this is only part of revival. Revival occurs when we are filled to overflowing with the Holy Spirit. This is the only way we can live lives of victory. If someone asked you right now, "Are you filled with the Holy Spirit?" What answer would you give? How many of us would be bold enough to answer, "Yes, I am filled with the Holy Spirit!" Revival occurs when we can say "Yes" at any moment of the day. We cannot say this in our own strength. We cannot fill ourselves with the Holy Spirit. Only God Himself can fill us to overflowing with His own Spirit. It is God's work from start to finish. We can be filled because of His grace. All we have to do is to give our broken, empty self to Him. He will fill it— and keep on filling it.

Here is an illustration the great preacher Andrew Murray used. Water will always look for the lowest place it can fill. In the same way, when God sees that you are low and empty before Him, He will fill you with His glory and power. Here is another picture which has made this truth simple and clear to many of us. Think of the human heart as a cup. We hold it out to the Lord Jesus, for we long that He should fill it with the Water of Life. The Lord Jesus is the Man who carries the golden water pot filled with the Water of Life. He looks into our cup. If it is clean, He fills it to overflowing with the Water of Life. As He is always with us, our cup can always be running over. This is what David meant when he sang: "My cup is overflowing." This is true revival. Our hearts are overflowing with blessing. The peace of God is continually ruling in our hearts. We are able to share these blessings with others.

Many people think that they will be sad if they die to self. This is not true. We are sad if we do *not* die to self. The more we know about dying with Christ, the more we shall know of His life, His peace, and His joy. His life will overflow from us to others. We shall want to see lost souls brought to Him. We shall want to see our fellow Christians filled with God's blessing.

Under the Blood

There is only one thing which stops the Lord Jesus from keeping our cups full. That thing is sin—sin in all its thousand forms. The Lord Jesus does not fill dirty cups. Anything which comes from self, however small it may be, is sin. If we try to serve God in our own strength, that is sin. If we think that we, by ourselves, are really doing well, that is sin. If we think we are being badly treated, that is sin. To pity ourselves is sin. It is sin to seek one's own way in business or Christian work. It is sin to spend one's spare time to please one's self. It is sin to get angry because someone has spoken against us. It is sin to resent it when others do better than we do. It is sin to strike back when others hurt us. It is sin to put self first, and to think of ourselves instead of thinking of the Lord. It is sin to hold back when God tells us to go on. It is sin to worry. It is sin to fear anything but God. All these things come from self and make our cups unclean.

You may think this is wrong. You may say that some of these things are not really sins. You may say that everyone pities himself, and all people are afraid of some things. "They are just weaknesses which all people have. They are things which disable us. They are part of the way we are made. It is wrong to call them sins. This would make us like slaves," you may say. But this is not true. If these things are not sins, then we must live with them all our lives. We cannot hope to be saved from them. But if these things and others like them are sins, we know that we can be saved from them. We know that the Lord Jesus died to save us from our sins. If, as soon as we realize that any of these things are in us, we confess them to Him and so put them "under His blood," we may be saved and cleansed from them. They really are sins. They come from unbelief. They are, strange to say, a form of pride. Many, many times these things have stopped the Lord Jesus from working in us and showing Himself through us.

All of our sins—the ones we all know are sins and the ones which some may call weaknesses—were put into another cup. That was the cup from which the Lord Jesus shrank for a moment in the Garden of Gethsemane. But on the cross He drank every drop in it. That was the cup of our sin. If we let Him do it, He will show us the sin in our cups. We must then confess it to Him. He will cleanse our hearts in His blood, which He shed for our sins. This does not mean just to cleanse us from the guilt of sin. It means that He cleanses us from the stain and dirt of sin, so that we no longer feel guilty of sin (Hebrews 10:2). As the Lord Jesus makes our cups clean, He fills them to overflowing with His Holy Spirit.

Each day we are able to take for ourselves the cleansing of His precious blood. You may have trusted the Lord Jesus to cleanse your cup and fill it to overflowing. Then some sin comes along—envy or anger. What happens? Your cup becomes dirty. It stops overflowing. If we are always being defeated by sin, our cup will never be overflowing.

So if we want always to know revival in our lives, we must learn the way to keep our cups clean. It is never God's will that revival should cease. He is not pleased when we speak of the revival which happened in such and such a year. Why was there no revival in the years in between? There can be only one reason—that is *sin*. The little sins which Satan drops into our cups hinder revival. What must we do? We must go back to Calvary. We must learn afresh that the blood of Jesus can cleanse us, moment by moment, from the beginning of sin. If we do this, we have learned the secret of having our cups always clean and always overflowing. As soon as you know that there is some little sin—envy, criticism, annoyance, whatever it is—give it to the Lord Jesus. Confess it to Him. He will cleanse it away by the power of His blood. The sin which comes from self will be taken away. You will again have joy and peace. Your cup will again be running over. The more you come for cleansing, the less will self be able to cause you to sin.

But before we can be made clean, our wills must be broken before God about this matter. There may be something in someone else's nature which annoys us. It is not enough to take this reaction of annoyance to the cross. First of all, we must yield ourselves to God about this whole matter. We must accept that person, with all his or her nature, as God's will for us. Only then can we take the wrong feelings which we have to the Lord Jesus. As we confess them to Him, we know He will cleanse us by His blood. After He has made us clean, there is no more need to be sad about that sin. We do not need to keep on thinking about ourselves. No, we should look to our Lord, the Victorious One, and praise Him because He is still the Victor.

The Word of God gives us one simple rule to show us how to walk with the Lord Jesus. This rule covers all our lives. It will always show us when sin has come in. It is found in Colossians 3:15: "The peace that Christ gives is to be the judge in your hearts."

Anything which spoils the peace which Christ gives us is sin. It may be a very small thing. It may, at first, not look like sin at all. The peace which Christ gives is our judge. This "judge" is like the referee in a game of football. If he sees any player break a rule of the game, he blows his whistle. The game has to stop, and cannot go on again until he allows it. When we lose our peace, it means that the referee Christ has placed in our hearts has blown his whistle! We should stop at once, and ask God to show us what is wrong. He will show us the sin which has come in. We must confess this to Him, and then that sin will be washed away by the blood of the Lord Jesus. We shall again have peace in our hearts. We shall go away with our cups running over.

But what if Christ does not give us His peace again? This means that our wills have not really been broken. Perhaps we have to confess that we have done wrong to someone else as well as to God. Perhaps we still think that the other person has done wrong. He or she *may* have done so, but if we have lost *our* peace it shows that *we* have done wrong. We do not lose our peace with God because of another person's sin. We lose it only because of our own sin. God wants to show us what our real self is like, and how it acts. We will only have God's peace in our hearts when we are willing to let Him cleanse us from our sins.

It is a very simple thing to be ruled by the peace which Christ gives us, but it is also a very searching thing. We can keep *nothing* hidden from God's Holy

Spirit, and it is the Holy Spirit through whom God gives us His peace. Before, we may never have worried about some of our selfish ways. But now God shows them to us as sins in His sight. We cannot walk in these ways now without the referee blowing His whistle. When we are ready to be ruled each day by the peace of God, we shall see that grumbling, trying to rule others, carelessness, and many other "little" faults are really sins. Many times a day, over very little things, we shall have to take for our own the cleansing power of the blood of the Lord Jesus. Our wills will be broken in a way that they were not broken before. Each day we will find ourselves living like this. But in our brokenness the Lord Jesus will show Himself in all His loveliness and grace.

But many of us have failed to listen for the referee's whistle for so long that we can no longer hear it. Day after day we feel that we have little need to be made clean from sin. We do not think we need to be broken before God. If we are like this, then our real spiritual state is probably much worse than we think. We need to have a real hunger for fellowship with God. This hunger must really fill our hearts and lives. Only then will we be ready to cry to God to ask Him to show us the sin in our life. Only then can the cleansing power of the blood of the Lord Jesus be made real to us. At first, God may show us just one thing that must be put right. As we obey Him, and are broken before Him on that one thing, we shall take the first step into real revival for us.

Chapter 3

THE WAY OF FELLOWSHIP———

W HEN GOD made man, He made him to have fellowship with Himself. But when man fell into sin, he made himself, not God, the center of his life. In this way man's fellowship with God was broken. But that was not all. Sin meant that man's fellowship with his fellow man was also broken. In the third chapter of Genesis we read how man had his first quarrel with God. In the very next chapter we read how man had his first quarrel with his fellow man. The result of that quarrel was that Cain murdered his brother Abel. "We . . . left God's paths to follow our own" (Isaiah 53:6). That is just what the fall of man means. If I want my own way rather than God's way, I shall also want my own way rather than another man's way. When a man says, "I am independent: I do not need to obey God," he will certainly not want to obey his fellow man, unless he is forced to do it. What is the result? A world in which every man wants his own way must, by its own nature, be a world full of trouble and war. When each man wants his own way, he will be angry with others when they do not let him have it. He will make walls to divide himself from others and will have bad thoughts about them. He will have wrong ideas about why they do some things. This will cause men to fight each other. We see all of these things in the world today.

What did the Lord Jesus Christ do when He died on the cross? Why did He give His life for us? He died to bring men back into fellowship with God. But that is not all. He gave His life to bring men back into fellowship with their fellow men. Both things must happen at once: we cannot have one without the other. As the spokes of a wheel get nearer and nearer to the hub, they get nearer and nearer to each other as well! So if we do not enjoy living fellowship with our brother in Christ, it shows that we do not enjoy living fellowship with God. We find this clearly taught in John's first letter. When we know revival in our own lives, we can really understand what John is teaching in this letter. John shows that we can only test how deep and real a man's fellowship with God is by seeing how deep and real his fellowship is with his brethren (1 John 2:9; 3:14–15; 4:20). These two things are so closely related that it is impossible to separate them. Anything which comes as a wall to divide us from another—however small it may be— also comes as a wall between us and God. We must put these things right immediately and take away the wall. If we do not do this, these walls will get thicker and thicker. It will seem as if we are shut off from God and our brother by thick stone walls. Some of us have learned these things from God. This means that if we want His new life to come to us, it will show itself by a walk of oneness with God and our brother, with no walls to divide us.

Light and Darkness

How can we have real fellowship with God and our brother? The answer is found in 1 John 1:7. *"If we live in the light—just as he is in the light—then we have fellowship with one another, and the blood of Jesus, his Son, makes us clean from all our sins."* These are words which have come to us with fresh meaning. What is the difference between light and darkness? Light enables us to see things; darkness hides them. Anything which shows us what we really are is light! "When all things are brought out to the light, then their true nature is clearly revealed; for anything that is clearly revealed becomes light" (Ephesians 5:13–14). But when we in any way try to hide what we are or what we have done, that is darkness. We may do this in different ways—by doing something, or saying something, or *not* saying something—but it is still darkness.

The first thing which sin in our lives will make us do is to hide what we are. When our first parents knew that they had sinned, they hid behind the trees of the garden. Sin has had the same effect on all of us ever since. When we have sinned, we try to hide it in some way. We cannot show our real self, so we pretend to be different from what we are. We say one thing to someone and a different thing to someone else. We like to make things look better than they are. We excuse ourselves and put the blame on others. We can all do this by being silent as well as by saying or doing something. This is what John in the previous verse calls "living in the darkness." Perhaps the sin is only being self-conscious: but, remember, everything that comes from self is sin! Perhaps we hide it by pretending to be what we are not. Even this is living in the darkness.

Verse 5 of this chapter tells us that "God is light." This means that God is the one who can show each man as he really is. It goes on to say that "there is no darkness at all in him" (1 John 1:5). There is nothing in God which can allow us to try to hide anything from Him.

This makes it very clear that we cannot have fellowship with God if we try to live in any way in the darkness. And while we are living in the darkness, we cannot have true fellowship with our brother either. The reason is that we are not real with him, and no one can have fellowship with someone who is not real. There is a wall, made by self, which divides him and us.

The Only Way to Have Fellowship

The only way we can have true fellowship with God and man is to live in the open with both. "If we live in the light—just as he is in the light—then we have fellowship with one another." To live in the light is just the opposite of living in the darkness. In one of his sermons the great English preacher Charles

Spurgeon said that walking in the light meant that we were willing to know and to be known. In our relationship with God, this means that we are willing to know the whole truth about ourselves. We are ready for Him to show us things which do not please Him. As soon as our conscience shows us that we have done something wrong, we are ready to obey God. If He shows us that something is sin, we shall deal with it as sin. We shall not try to hide anything, or pretend that it is not true. If we live in the light like this, we are sure to find more and more sin in our lives. We shall find that things which before we did not think to be sins are really sins. That is why we may be afraid to live in the light. We may think it best to go on living, at least to some extent, in the darkness. But our verse goes on to tell us the wonderful truth that "the blood of Jesus, his Son, makes us clean from all our sins." When God's light shows us that something is sin, we can confess it to Him. Then we know that the blood of the Lord Jesus will make us clean from this sin. The sin will be gone— gone from God's sight and gone from our hearts. The precious blood of Christ can make us whiter than snow. As we live in the light and are made clean by the blood, we have fellowship with God.

Here God promises us, however, not only that we can have fellowship with Him if we live in the light, but also that we can have fellowship with one another. This means that we must walk in the light with our brother as well. We cannot be "in the light" with God, and "in the darkness" with our brother. We must be as willing to know the truth about ourselves from our brother as to know it from God. We must be ready to let him hold the light to us, and we must be ready in the same way to hold the light to him. If our brother sees anything in our lives which is not the best for God, we must be ready to listen to him tell us in love about it. We must be willing to know ourselves for what we really are, and we must be willing for our brother to know this as well. We will not hide our inner selves from those with whom we should be in fellowship. We will not pretend to be different from what we really are. We will not cover our faults. We will speak the truth about ourselves with them. We will be ready to give up our spiritual privacy. We will not be proud, but will be willing to have people say bad things about us so that we can be open and truthful with our brethren in Christ. We will not keep bad feelings in our hearts about another person. We will first of all ask God to save us from them. Then we shall go and put it right with the ones concerned. As we live in this way, we shall find that we shall have greater and deeper fellowship with one another. We shall not love one another less, but far, far more.

No Slavery

To live in the light means simply to live with the Lord Jesus. There is no slavery about that! This does not mean that we have to tell everyone everything about ourselves. But it does mean that we have to *live*, day by day, in the light. Are we ready to be open with our brother, and tell him so, when God tells us to do so? Paul writes: "Let us take up the weapons for fighting in the light" (Romans 13:12). To do this will sometimes make us humble. But it will help us to know Christ, and to know ourselves, in a new and real way. We say we know that God knows all about us, but we do not really grasp what this means. As a result we do not know the truth about ourselves. But what will happen if, with God's guidance, we tell the real truth about ourselves to one other person? We shall come to know our sins and ourselves in a way which we never knew before. We shall begin to see more clearly than ever before where the redemption in Christ needs to be applied more and more to our lives. That is why James tells us to confess our sins to one another (James 5:16).

1 John 1:7 tells us to "live in the light" so that we can "have fellowship with one another." As we walk this way together, we can have wonderful fellowship. As each one is ready for the other to know him or her as a repentant sinner before the Cross, each one will truly love the other. When the walls which divide us are taken away, and the disguises that cover us are taken away, God can really make us one. There is another joy in this fellowship. We know that we are "safe" with each other. We know that the others will not have hard thoughts about us which they are hiding from us. We know that, if we have truly agreed to live in fellowship in the light of the Cross, any such thoughts will be brought into the light. The person who has had them will be bro-

ken before the Cross, and confess his sin and lack of love. Sometimes he may have to bring to our notice something about ourselves which we ought to know.

But let us remember that our living in the light is above all a life with the Lord Jesus. We must settle things with Him first of all. We must first let Him make our hearts clean. We must receive the victory from Him. Then, when God guides us to open our hearts to others, we shall be able to tell them what God has done for us. If we have done something wrong to others, that must of course be confessed. Then we shall be able to praise God together.

Teams of Two for Revival

Today the Lord Jesus wants you to begin, in a new way, to live in the light with Him. Join with one other person: your Christian friend, the person you live with, your wife or your husband. Take off the disguise. God has, I am sure, shown you something, more than any other thing, which you should be open about with him or her. Start there. Be a team of two to work for revival among the believers with whom you meet. As others are broken at the Cross, God will bring them into this deeper fellowship with you. Meet together from time to time to have fellowship together, and to share your spiritual experiences. Be open with each other. Pray together for others. Go out together and tell others what God has done for you. God will begin to work in a wonderful way through such a group. As He saves others, and brings them into this living blessing, they can begin to have fellowship together and work in this same way. Just as a spark from one fire can begin another fire, so one group can cause another group to begin. In this way, right through the whole land, there will be people who know the meaning of New Life from our risen Lord Jesus.

Chapter 4

___THE HIGHWAY OF HOLINESS

I T IS REALLY a very simple thing to live a victorious Christian life. We must learn this. We have made it sound very hard and complicated. People have written big books about it. Some have used all kinds of long words which ordinary people cannot understand. Others tell us that this is the secret, or that is the secret, and so on. This makes it seem so complicated that most of us, while we have some book knowledge of holiness, cannot relate it to our day-by-day living. In this chapter we want to make as clear as possible the simple truths that we have been thinking about. We shall therefore set them out in the form of a picture.

The Highway

We read about the Highway in Isaiah 35:8 and 9. These verses have helped many of us to get an overall picture of the life of victory. "A main road will go through that once deserted land; it will be named, 'The Holy Highway.'" The picture is of a highway going through the muddy land of the world. The

Highway is narrow and goes uphill, but it is possible for us to walk it. "Even the most stupid cannot miss the way." There are dangers if we get off the road, but if we keep on the Highway we are safe. "No lion will lurk along its course, nor will there be any other dangers." But "no evil-hearted man may walk upon it." No sinner who does not know Christ as His Saviour can walk on this road. The Christian who is living in sin cannot walk there either. He is keeping evil in his heart, that is, he is not confessing it to the Lord and being made clean by Him.

There is only one way to get on this Highway. We must go up the small dark Hill of Calvary. We must climb this hill on our hands and knees—especially our knees. We will not do this if we are content with our present Christian life. We must have a real hunger in our hearts to get on the Highway. Then only will we get on our knees and begin to climb the hill. Only those who are not satisfied—who are hungry—will really do this. Do not hurry. Let God give you a real hunger to get on the Highway. Let Him really make you pray to know Him. You will not get far if you only want to look, and then go away again. "You will find me when you seek me, if you look for me in earnest" (Jeremiah 29:13).

A Low Door

At the top of the hill, guarding the way to the Highway, stands the cross. The cross is the place of death. It marked the end of this life for all those who were nailed to it. It divides time into two parts. It divides men into two groups. At the foot of the cross is a low door. This is the only way to get on the Highway. The door is so low that a person must stoop down and crawl through it. But unless we do this we shall never go any further. This door is the Door of the Broken Ones. Only those who have been broken can go on the Highway. To be broken means to be "no longer I . . . but . . . Christ" (Galatians 2:20).

In each one of us there is a proud, stiff-necked self. This began in the Garden of Eden. Adam and Eve at first used to bow their heads to obey God's will. Then they broke His command. They made their necks stiff. They wanted independence. They tried to be like gods. All through the Bible we find the same thing. God told His people time and time again that they had stiff necks. The same is true of us. We are hard and do not want to give up our rights. We become sad and feel hurt when people say bad things about us. We become angry. We want things that other people have. We say unkind things about them. We are sad when they get on well. We are not ready to forgive. We try in our own strength to do things that only God can do for us. We try to please ourselves—and this often leads to our doing unclean things. Each one of these things—and many more—come from the proud self inside us. If this self were not there and Christ were in its place, we would not act as we do.

If we want to enter the Highway, God must bend and break our stiff-necked self. Only then can Christ reign in its stead. To be broken means that we have no rights before God and men. It does not mean just giving up our rights to God. It means that we have no rights at all! The one right we have is to go to hell! It means to be nothing. It means to have nothing I can call my own. It means that all we have—our time, our money, our goods, our positions—belong to God.

How can God break our wills, so that we want His will and not our own? He brings us to the foot of the cross. There He shows us what it really means to be broken. We see the wounded hands and feet of the Son of God. We see His head crowned with thorns. We see the complete brokenness of the One who prayed, "Not my will, however, but your will be done" (Luke 22:42). He drank the dark, bitter cup of our sins to the last drop. This is the way to be broken. We must look on Him and realize that it was our sin which nailed Him to the cross. There we see the love and brokenness of the Son of God. There He died in our place. As we look upon Him, our hearts will be strangely melted. We will want to be broken for Him. We shall pray from our hearts:

> *O to be saved from myself, dear Lord,*
> *O to be lost in Thee!*
> *O that it may be no more I,*
> *But Christ that lives in me.*

God always loves to answer our prayers. Some of us have found that this prayer—the prayer that He might break us—is the one that He answers more quickly than any other prayer.

We Must Always Choose to Be Broken

We must be broken as we go through the door. But this is not the only time. From then on, we must always choose to be broken. God will show us what He wants us to do, but we must choose to obey Him. Someone does something that hurts us. Perhaps they do not pay attention to us. What can we do? We can accept the hurt as a way God is using to make us humble. Or we can resist it. We can make our necks stiff again. But our spirits will be unhappy. Right through the day God will see whether we are really broken or not. If we are not broken to those around us, we are not broken before God. It is no use saying that we are. God nearly always tests us through others. We cannot say that a thing is *not* from God. God shows us His will in the things He allows to happen to us. He allows other people to come in contact with us. He tests us through them. You may find that you are not living in brokenness. If so, you must go back to Calvary. Look again on the Christ who was broken for you. You will come away willing to be broken for Him.

Over the Door of the Broken Ones there is sprinkled the precious blood of the Lord Jesus Christ. As we bend to crawl through the door, His blood makes us clean from all sin. We cannot get through without bending: only the clean can walk on the Highway. Perhaps you have never known the Lord Jesus as your Saviour. Perhaps you have known Him for years. But in either case you have been made unclean by sin. Sins like pride, envy, wrong feelings to others, and sexual sins have made you unclean. You must confess all these things to the Lord Jesus. He died on the cross to make you clean from them. If you give them to Him, He will softly say to you the words which He once said on the cross: "It is finished." Your heart will be made whiter than snow.

The Gift of His Fullness

This is the way to get on the Highway. From the cross we see it before us. It is a narrow uphill road. God's light shines on it and it leads to the heavenly Jerusalem. On both sides of the road there is thick darkness. The darkness comes to the very edge of the Highway. However, on the Highway itself there is light. Behind us we can see the cross. It no longer looks dark for now it glows with light. We no longer see the Lord Jesus hanging on the cross, dying for us. We see Him walking on the Highway. He is overflowing with His risen life. In His hands He carries the golden water pot filled with the Water of Life. He comes up to us and asks us to hold out our hearts to Him, just as if we were holding out a cup. We give our empty hearts to Him. He looks inside, and we may feel pain as we know that we can hide nothing from Him. But when He sees that we have allowed Him to cleanse them by His blood, He fills them with the Water of Life. We are filled to overflowing with His new life. This is real revival. You and I are filled, all the time, with the Holy Spirit. We love others. We long to see others saved as well. We are not fighting in our own strength. We are not waiting idly for God to act. We simply give to Him each sin, as soon as we are conscious of it. We confess it, and know that He will make us clean in His precious blood. We accept from His hands the free gift of His fullness. We allow Him to do His work through us. We walk along with Him. He is always there to fill our cups, so they are always overflowing.

The rest of our Christian life is simply to walk along the Highway. Our hearts overflow with the Water of Life. At all times we bow our heads to obey His will. We always trust in His blood to make us clean. We live in complete oneness with the Lord Jesus. There is nothing about this life which draws other people's attention to it. We do not need to feel sad if we do not have any wonderful emotional feelings. It is simply to live, day by day, the kind of life the Lord wants us to live. This is real holiness.

Away From the Highway

The Highway is narrow. We may, and sometimes do, slip off the Highway. If we take one little step aside, we are off the Highway and in darkness. How can this happen? It happens when we fail to obey God. It happens when we are not willing to be weak enough to let God work in us. Satan is always beside the road. He shouts at us, but remember, he cannot touch us. But by an act of our own wills we can yield to him. This is the beginning of sin. This will cause us to move away from the Lord Jesus.

Sometimes we make our necks stiff. This may be

to another person or to God Himself. Sometimes envy and wrong feelings to others come to attack us. Sometimes we try to fight in our own strength and do not rest in Him. At once we are away from the road. Our hearts are unclean—and nothing unclean can be on the Highway. Our cup is dirty and it stops overflowing. We lose our peace with God. We must get back on the Highway at once. If not, we shall go farther and farther away. But how can we get back? The first thing is to ask God to show us what caused us to get off the Highway. He will do this, though sometimes we are slow to see it.

Perhaps someone has annoyed me. I had wrong feelings about him or her. If I had been broken this would not have happened. I look back to the Highway, longing to be on it again. I see the Lord Jesus there. I see what an ugly thing it is to have wrong thoughts about another person. I see that the Lord Jesus died to save me from this. On hands and knees I crawl back to the Highway. I come to the Lord Jesus. I confess my sin and receive His cleansing. He is waiting to fill my cup to overflowing again.

Praise the Lord! No matter where you leave the Highway, He is there to call you back. He wants you to be broken again. He will make you clean once again in His precious blood. This is the great secret of the Highway. We must know what to do with sin when it comes in. We must always take it to the Cross. There we shall see its sinfulness. We must confess it to God. We must believe that He has taken it away because of the value of the blood of the Lord Jesus.

This then is the real test all along the Highway. Are our cups running over? Do we have the peace which God gives in our hearts? Have we real love for others? Are we concerned about them? These things show us whether we are really on the Highway or not. If our peace and love are out of order, sin has come in somewhere. It may be that we have pitied ourselves. We may have tried to get our own way. We may have tried to please ourselves in some way. We may have been upset at things others have said about us. We may have given these things a wrong meaning. We may have tried to defend ourselves. We may have been fighting in our own strength. We may have put ourselves first. We may have tried to hide ourselves. We may have worried about something or we may have been afraid. Any one of these things, and many others, can and will spoil our peace and our love.

Our Life With Others

We must say one other important thing about the Highway. We do not walk on it alone. Others walk with us. We know, of course, that the Lord Jesus is there. But there are other travelers as well. What is the rule of the road? Just as we have fellowship with the Lord Jesus, we must have fellowship with them as well. This is very important. These two kinds of fellowship are closely linked to each other. We cannot spoil one without spoiling the other. Anything which comes between us and another person comes between us and God. If we are impatient with another person or have wrong thoughts about him or envy him, this will be like a barrier between us and him. It may be like a thin curtain that we can still see through, but if it is not taken away at once it will get thicker. It will become like a blanket and then like a brick wall. These things shut us off from God and each other. We are shut in to ourselves. It is easy to see why these two relationships are so closely linked. God is love. He loves others. When we fail to love others, we put ourselves out of fellowship with God. The reason is that God still loves the other person even if we do not.

Such sins have another effect. They make us walk "in darkness" (1 John 2:9–11). They make us try to cover up and hide what we are really like. That is always the meaning "the darkness" in the Bible. The light shows the true state of affairs: the darkness hides it. The first effect of sin to make us hide. We pretend to be what we really are not. We wear a mask to hide our real selves. We are not real with either God or men. And neither God nor men can have fellowship with someone who is not real.

The way back to fellowship with the Lord Jesus will also bring us back into fellowship with our brother as well. Anything in us which does not come from love is sin. We must realize that it is sin and confess it as sin. Then alone can it be cleansed by the blood of the Lord Jesus. And then we can put things right with our brother as well. This is the way we must come back to the Lord Jesus. As we do this, we shall find His love for our brother filling our hearts.

We shall want to show our love by our actions toward him. Then we shall walk together in fellowship again.

This is the life of the Highway. It is not a new teaching. There is nothing surprising about it. It is not some new idea for us to preach about. It is a life which we must live every day, wherever the Lord has placed us. It is not against other things which you may have read or heard about the Christian life. We have simply put into picture language the great truths about how to be holy. If we start now to live in this way, we shall keep on having revival. Revival simply means this: you and I must walk along the Highway in true oneness with the Lord Jesus. This will mean oneness too with one another. He will keep our cups clean as we confess our sins to Him. Then He will fill them to overflowing with the love and the life of God.

Chapter
5

THE DOVE AND THE LAMB___

HOW CAN we live a life of victory? How can we do useful service for God? How can we win souls for Him? We cannot do these things by our own efforts. We cannot do them just by working hard. They are only the fruit of the Holy Spirit. A tree does not work to get fruit. Fruit grows on it. The fruit that grows on us must be the fruit of God's Holy Spirit. To bear this fruit we must be filled with the Holy Spirit. "The trees of the Lord should always be full of sap." Here "sap" is a picture of the Holy Spirit.

There is a wonderful picture of this in the first chapter of John's Gospel. John the Baptist saw the Lord Jesus coming toward him. He said about Him, "Here is the Lamb of God who takes away the sin of the world!" (John 1:29). What had happened when John baptized Him? John himself said: "I saw the Spirit come down like a dove from heaven and stay on him" (John 1:32).

The Humbleness of God

What thoughts does this picture bring to mind? The Dove came down from heaven and stayed on the Lamb! The lamb and the dove are two of the most gentle creatures God has made. The lamb is a picture of meekness and obedience. The dove always speaks of peace. The soft cooing of a dove is always a peaceful sound. Does not this suggest to us that there is humbleness in the very heart of God? The everlasting God has chosen to show Himself in His Son. He has given to His Son the name of the Lamb. When the Holy Spirit came into the world to stay on the Lord Jesus, He showed Himself as a dove. Why do we need to be humble to walk with God? It is true that God is so much bigger than we are that we should be humble. But that is not all. We see what God is like when we look at the Lord Jesus, and He is "gentle and humble in spirit" (Matthew 11:29).

What is the main lesson we should learn from this happening? The Dove, the Holy Spirit, could come down and stay on the Lord Jesus only because He was the Lamb. He had the nature of the Lamb. He was humble and obedient. He gave Himself fully to His Father. If He had had a different kind of nature, the Dove could never have rested on Him. The Dove has a gentle nature, and would have been afraid and flown away, if the Lord Jesus had not been gentle and humble in spirit.

Do we want the Holy Spirit to come and stay on us? Then we too must be gentle and humble in spirit.

The Dove can only stay on us when we are willing
to be like the Lamb. He cannot stay on us while our
self is not broken. The things which come from our
unbroken self are the very opposite to the gentle-
ness of the Dove. The fruit of the Spirit is described
in Galatians 5:22. "The Spirit produces love, joy,
peace, patience, kindness, goodness, faithfulness,
humility, and self-control." These are the things with
which the Dove desires to fill us! Look at the difference between these and the things that human nature does (see Galatians 5:19–21). The "flesh" is the
New Testament word for the unbroken self. It is like
a cruel, snarling wolf. The Holy Spirit is like the
gentle Dove!

The Nature of the Lamb

Do we want the Holy Spirit to come on us and
stay with us? Then we must be like the Lamb about
every matter which He shows to us. Let us look at
the Lamb on His way to Calvary. As we do so, we
shall also see clearly our own hearts. It will make us
humble to see how unlike Him we are. We shall see
how often we have *not* taken the place of the Lamb.

Let us look at Him for a moment as the Lamb. He
was the *simple* Lamb. A lamb is one of the simplest
of God's creatures. It makes no plans to help itself. It
is helpless. The Lord Jesus made Himself as nothing
for us. He became the simple Lamb. He had no
strength or wisdom of His own. He did not make
plans to get Himself out of trouble. At all times He

depended on His Father. "The Son does nothing on his own; he only does what he sees his Father doing" (John 5:19). But we are not simple! We make plans to help ourselves. We try in all kinds of ways to get ourselves out of trouble. We try to live the Christian life in our own strength. We try in our own strength to work for God. We think we are something, and can do something for God. If we are not willing to be simple lambs, how can God's Spirit stay on us? How can we know that He is living with us?

The Lamb Was Shorn

When a lamb is shorn, all its wool is cut off. This is what happened to the Lord Jesus. All His rights were taken away from Him. People took away His good name by saying bad things about Him. They took away His freedom. But He did not fight back. A lamb never does. "When he was cursed he did not answer back with a curse" (1 Peter 2:23). "When he suffered he did not threaten." He did not say: "You cannot do this to Me! Don't you know that I am the Son of God?" But what about us? How often have we been unwilling to be shorn of our rights? We have not been willing to lose our own rights for Him. We want people to honor us. We want good positions. We are ready to fight for them! The Dove has had to fly away. We have not been willing to be shorn lambs. We have been left without peace and without love because of our hard hearts.

He Gave No Answer

The Lord Jesus was also the *silent* Lamb. "As a sheep before her shearers is dumb, so he stood silent . . ." (Isaiah 53:7). When men were shouting for His death, He gave no answer. He never defended Himself. He did not explain what He had done. But what about us? What have we done when other people have said unkind or untrue things about us? Have *we* been silent? No, we have answered in loud voices. We have defended ourselves. We have tried to show that we have been right. We have gotten angry. When we should have honestly admitted we were wrong, we have tried to show that we were not. When this happens, the Dove must fly away. We cannot know His presence and blessing, because we have not been willing to be the silent lamb.

No Bad Feelings Toward Others

The Lord Jesus was also the *spotless* Lamb. He did not say anything bad. He did not have any bad feelings toward others. There was nothing but love in His heart for the men who sent Him to the cross. He did not want to harm them in return. There were no bad and bitter feelings in His heart. He forgave them even while they were putting the nails in His hands. He asked His Father to forgive them as well. He willingly and humbly suffered for us. But what about us? People have not treated us nearly so badly as they treated the Lord Jesus. But what bad and bitter feelings we have had! What wrong thoughts we have had toward different ones! These things have made our hearts unclean. Because we were not willing to bear it and forgive it for Jesus' sake, the Dove has had to fly away.

Come Back, O Dove!

These are the things which drive the Dove away. They stop us from enjoying His blessings. They are all sins. Sin is the only thing which can stop revival. The great question which we must ask is this: "How can the Dove come back to our lives with His grace and power?" The answer is this: "The Lamb of God." We have seen that He is the simple, shorn, silent, and spotless Lamb. But this is not all. He is, above all else, the *substitute* Lamb.

Why did the Jews offer lambs in sacrifice to God? Was it because lambs are meek and obedient animals? This was not the real reason. The lamb was offered on the altar as a substitute for the one who offered it. The lamb had to be killed. Its blood was sprinkled on the altar to atone for sin. That was why the Lord Jesus made Himself the *humble* Lamb. He died on the cross as our Substitute. He was the Sacrifice for our sins. "Christ himself carried our sins on his body to the cross" (1 Peter 2:24). He died to forgive our sins and to make us clean from them. We receive these things when we really turn from our sins. That is why God wants to take us back to the Cross. There we see our sins wounding and causing pain to the Lamb. In an old Negro spiritual, this

question is asked: "Were you there when they crucified my Lord?" The answer is: "Yes, we were." We
have been unwilling to be broken. This shows that
we were part of the crowd which caused His death
on the cross. Our gentle Lamb was willing to let them
and us put Him to death. He shed His precious blood
for us. When we repent, He forgives our sins and
makes us clean from them. May this solemn thought
cause our proud hearts to break in repentance! We
must see that these sins caused the Lord Jesus to die
for us. We must be really broken, and repent of them.
Then we can put them right. Then alone the blood
of the Lamb will cleanse us from these sins. And then
the Dove will come back and bring peace and blessing to our hearts.

> *He humbled Himself to the manger,*
> *And even to Calvary's tree;*
> *But I am so proud and unwilling,*
> *His humble disciple to be.*
>
> *He yielded His will to the Father,*
> *And chose to abide in the Light;*
> *But I prefer wrestling to resting*
> *And try by myself to do right.*
>
> *Lord, break me, then cleanse me and fill me,*
> *And keep me abiding in Thee;*
> *That fellowship may be unbroken*
> *And Thy Name be kept holy in me.*

An African Christian, a real follower of the Lord Jesus, once told the people to whom he was preaching this story. He was climbing a hill to go to the meeting. He heard the sound of footsteps behind him. He turned and saw a Man climbing up behind him. The Man was carrying a very heavy load on His back. The Christian felt very sorry for Him. He spoke to Him. Then he noticed the Man's hands. They were scarred! He realized that the Man was the Lord Jesus. The African said to Him: "Lord, are You carrying the world's sin up the hill?" "No, not the world's sin. Only yours!" the Lord Jesus replied.

As the African told the vision which God had given him, his heart and the hearts of those who were listening to him were broken. They saw their sins at the cross. Our hearts need to be broken in the same way. When this happens, we shall truly turn from our sins. We shall be ready to confess them to God and to others against whom we have done wrong. We shall be ready to become one with others again. We shall give back anything which we have wrongly taken from another. When we have humbled ourselves, as the Lord Jesus humbled Himself, the Dove will come back to us. We shall again know His peace and His love.

> Return, O heavenly Dove, return,
>   Sweet Messenger of rest!
> I hate the sins that made Thee mourn,
>   And drove Thee from my breast.

Ruled by the Dove

One last word. The dove is the symbol of peace. If the blood of Jesus has made us clean, and if we are humbly walking with the Lamb, the sign that the Holy Spirit is living in us in all His fullness will be peace. This is to be the test of our life all along the way. "The peace that Christ gives is to be the judge in your hearts" (Colossians 3:15). If the Dove stops singing in our hearts, that is, if our peace is broken, it must be because of sin. In some matter we have not been humble like the Lamb. We must ask God to show us what it was. We must quickly turn from it. We must confess that sin and bring it to the Cross. Then the Dove will again have His right place in our hearts. Again we shall experience the peace of God. This is the only way we can know that the Holy Spirit is always living and ruling in our hearts. We are sinful men and women. We have fallen into sin. But if we confess each sin as soon as we know we have committed it, we are made clean by the blood of Jesus. And the Dove will rest on our lives.

What must we do about it? From this day on, let us allow the peace which Christ gives to be the judge in our hearts. Let us allow the Heavenly Dove to rule our lives, each moment of every day. If we do this, we shall find, each day, more and more things in our lives which are sin in God's sight. We shall be made very humble. But this is the only way we can be made like the Lamb of God. This is the only way that self can be conquered. This is the only way to live a life of real victory.

Chapter 6

_____REVIVAL IN THE HOME

THOUSANDS of years ago there was a most beautiful garden. The world has never seen another garden like it. In that garden there lived a man and a woman. God had made them in His own likeness. They lived to show Him to the other things He had made, and to each other. Each moment of each day they lived to bring glory to Him. They knew that God was their Creator; they knew that they were creatures which He had made. Every day they did what He wanted them to do. They humbly accepted this as their real position. They lived for God and not for themselves. Each gladly did what the other wanted to do. In that first home in the garden there was true peace, love, and oneness with God and with each other.

But one day that peace was broken. Satan in the form of a snake came into that home. Until this time, God was the center of the lives of that man and woman. But when they listened to Satan instead of to God, sin came in. They lost their peace and fellowship with God—and with each other. They were no longer living for God. Each one now lived for self. They had become their own gods. They no longer lived for each other. Their peace, love, and oneness were gone. In their place was disagreement and hatred. *Sin* had come in!

Revival Begins in the Home

Sin first came into the home. We probably sin more often in our homes than anywhere else. That is why we first need revival in our homes. We need revival in the church. We need revival in our country. We need revival in the world. But we cannot pretend that we have revival in the church until we have it in our homes. The home is the hardest place to begin. It will cost us more here than anywhere else. But this is the place where we *must* begin.

Before we talk more about this, we must remember what revival really is. Revival is new life in hearts where the spiritual life has grown weak. It is not something which we can do, or even begin, by ourselves. It is not man's life. It is God's life. It is the life of the Lord Jesus filling us and flowing through us. That life is shown by fellowship and oneness with those with whom we live. There is no barrier between us and God, nor between us and others. The home is the most important place where we should experience this.

But is this our experience? Are we really like this in our homes? Do we get upset about little things? Do we easily get angry? Do we want our own way? Do we have hard thoughts about others? Perhaps we do not know of anything really wrong between us, but we are not really one. We do not know the full oneness and fellowship which should be true where Christians live together. The things which come between us and others also come between us and God. They spoil our fellowship with Him. They mean that our hearts are not filled to overflowing with God's life.

What is the real trouble? First of all, what do we mean by a home? We are talking about the relationships of man and wife, parents and children, and brothers and sisters. It also applies to others who for different reasons have to live together.

The first thing which is wrong with many families is that they are not open with each other. There are curtains between them. Others do not know what we are really like. We do not want them to know! Those who are living most closely with us do not know what is going on in our hearts. They do not know our troubles and battles. They do not know our failures. They do not know things from which the Lord Jesus has most often to make us clean. We hide ourselves in this way for one reason—*sin!* What was the first thing that Adam and Eve did after they sinned? They tried to hide from God behind the trees of the garden. Before that they had not tried to hide anything from God or from each other. Now they were hiding from God, and we know that this meant they would soon hide things from each other. Eve would not be allowed to know all the ideas and thoughts in Adam's mind. Adam would not know the things hidden in Eve's mind. It has been like this ever since. When we have something to hide from God, we hide it from each other as well. It is as if we put a mask on to hide our real face. We cover our real selves. We pretend to be happy when we are not. We are afraid to be really in earnest. We do not want others to get close and see us as we really are. So we pretend all the time. We are not real with each other. No one can have fellowship with an unreal person. That is why we cannot have real oneness and fellowship in the home. This is what the Bible calls "living in the darkness." Darkness is anything which hides.

We Fail to Love Each Other

What is the second thing which is wrong with our homes? We fail to really love one another. You may say: "That is not true in our home. No one could love one another any more than my husband and I love each other." But think for a moment. What do you mean by love? Love is not just an emotion. It is not the same as a strong sexual passion. In 1 Corinthians 13 the Apostle Paul tells us what real love is like. Let us test ourselves by this portion of the Bible. We may find, after all, that we do not love each other very much. Perhaps we do just the opposite of the things this chapter tells us to do. This means that, instead of loving, we are really hating each other! Let us look at some of the things which this chapter tells us about love. "Love is patient and kind; love is not jealous, or conceited, or proud; love is not ill-mannered, or selfish, or irritable; love does not keep a record of wrongs" (1 Corinthians 13:4–5).

What do these tests show about our life in the home? Very often we act in the very opposite way.

"Love is patient and kind." We are often impatient with one another. We are often unkind in the way we answer back or react when someone has said or done something which we do not like.

"Love is not jealous." But often there is jealousy in the home. A husband can be jealous of his wife's gifts. She can be jealous of his gifts. They can even be jealous of each other's spiritual progress! Parents may be jealous of their children. Very often there is bitter jealousy between brothers and sisters.

"Love is not conceited or proud." But we often are! Our conceit is shown in all sorts of little ways. We think we know best. We want our own way. We find fault with the other person. We give orders in the wrong way. If we do these things, we find that we look down on the other person. We think we are better than he or she is. If we really think like this, we shall blame him or her for everything. Yet we still say that we love!

"Love is not ill-mannered." Are we polite in our homes? Politeness is love in little things. So often we fail in little things. We think that we do not need to be as careful at home as we are outside.

"Love is not selfish." But many times a day we put our wishes, and the things we want to do, before those of the other one.

"Love is not irritable." But how quickly we can

become irritable! How often do we have unkind thoughts? How often do we feel angry because the other one has done something we did not want him to do, or has not done something we did want him to do? Yet we say that there is no lack of love in our homes!

These things happen every day and we think nothing of them. But they are all the opposite of love. And, remember, the opposite of love is hate. Impatience is hate. Envy is hate. Conceit and pride are hate. Selfishness is hate. To keep a record of wrongs is hate. And hate is *sin*. "Whoever says that he is in the light, yet hates his brother, is in the darkness to this very hour" (1 John 2:9). Living in the darkness causes wrong thoughts and makes barriers between us. We cannot have fellowship with God. We cannot have fellowship with one another.

The Only Way Back

We must ask ourselves one question. "Do I want new life, revival, in my own home?" Do we *really* want it? We must ask the question with our whole heart. Are we happy to go on as we are? Or have we got a real hunger for new life? Do we want to see God's life in our home? Unless we have a real desire for this, we shall not do what needs to be done. What is this? I must first of all call my own sin, *sin*. (The first step concerns me and my sin, not the other person and his or her sin.) I must take this to the Cross. I must confess it to the Lord Jesus. I must trust Him, then and there, to make me clean from this sin.

As we bow our heads at the Cross and see how the Lord Jesus forgot Himself and gave Himself to die because of His love for us, His love, patience, and kindness will flow into our hearts. His precious blood makes us clean from our lack of love and our unkind thoughts. The Holy Spirit fills us with the very nature of the Lord Jesus. In 1 Corinthians 13 we really have a description of the nature of the Lord Jesus. God is ready to give His nature to us, if Christ belongs to us. Each time we see that sin is beginning to creep in, we must confess it to Him. He will make us clean. More and more He will give His own nature to us.

But to do this, we must give ourselves to walking in the Way of the Cross in our homes. Many times we shall have to give up our rights, just as the Lord Jesus did for us. When people act selfishly and we act selfishly back, we shall see that it is *our* selfishness which is the real trouble. When people are proud and we become proud in turn, we shall see that *our* pride is the real trouble. We must see our own selfishness and pride as sin. We must take our sin to the Lord Jesus and be made clean. We must accept the way the other person does things as God's will for us. We must humbly bow to all that God allows to come into our lives. This does not mean that we should accept another person's selfishness as God's will for him or her. This is certainly *not* true. We must, however, accept it as God's will for us. When we are broken, God may want to use us to help the other person to see his or her need. If we are parents, we shall need to use firmness when we correct our children. But we must not do it from self-ish motives. We must do it because we love them and want them to be the best for God. We must at all times give up our rights to do what we want to do. This is the only way in which the love of the Lord Jesus will be able to fill us and show itself through us.

When we have been broken at Calvary, we must be willing to put things right with others. If we have done something wrong to our children, we must put it right with them too. This is very often the real test of our brokenness. Brokenness is the opposite of hardness. Hardness will say: "It's your fault!" Bro-kenness, however, says: "It's my fault!" If we are ready and willing to say that, things will be different in our homes. We must remember that at the Cross there is room for only one at a time. We can-not say: "I was wrong, but you were wrong too. You must come as well!" We must go alone and confess that *we* were wrong. We must be broken about the matter. God will work through our brokenness more than through anything else we can do or say. But we may have to wait. It may be a long time. But this will help us to understand how God Himself feels. Some-one has said something like this: "There was no wrong on God's side towards man. But 1,900 years ago God made His great attempt to put things right. He is still waiting for men to put things right from their side!"

God *will* answer our prayer. He will bring the

other person to the Cross as well. There we shall be one. The wall which divides us will be broken down. We shall be able to walk in the light. We shall "love one another earnestly with all [our] hearts" (1 Peter 1:22). Sin is one thing which all of us have. The only place where we can be really one is at the feet of Jesus, where our sins are washed away. Where two or more sinners meet together at Calvary, we see real oneness.

Chapter 7

THE SPECK AND THE LOG_____

OUR FRIEND has got something in his eye. It is only a tiny speck, but it is very painful. Until it is taken out, he cannot do anything to help himself. If we are his friends, it is surely our job to do all that we can to take it out. He should be very grateful to us for doing it. If we got a speck in our own eye and he helped to take it out, we too should be grateful to him.

We must keep this in mind as we think of the words of the Lord Jesus in Matthew 7:3–5. The Lord Jesus is *not* saying that we should not help others to get rid of their faults. No, he wants us to do this, no matter what the cost is to ourselves. At first, the Lord Jesus seems to call people who try to help others impostors. But this is not the case. He just wants us to get rid of our own faults first! Then we can really help others. We see this at the end of the passage: "You will be able to see and take the speck out of your brother's eye." The New Testament teaches us that we *should* care for others. We *should* do all we can to take out from the eyes of others the specks which stop them from seeing well and experiencing God's blessings. We are told to "teach one another" (Romans 15:14). "Let us . . . help one another to show love and to do good" (Hebrews 10:24). "Let us encourage one another" (Hebrews 10:25). "You, then, should wash each other's feet," said the Lord Jesus to His disciples (John 13:14). The love which the Lord Jesus has poured out upon us will make us want to help our brother in this way.

God may lead us humbly to bring some matter to the notice of a fellow believer. This can lead to great blessing, not only to the person we speak to, but to others as well. Dr. Tauler was a popular preacher in the city of Strasburg. In Basle, Switzerland, there was a humble Christian called Nicholas. He was a member of the Society of the Friends of God. He crossed the mountains, visited Dr. Tauler in his church, and said to him: "Dr. Tauler, there is something you must do before you can do your greatest work for God. You must die. You must die to yourself and your gifts and your popularity and even your own goodness. You must learn the full meaning of the Cross. When you do this, you will have new power with God and men." When Dr. Tauler heard this call from this little-known Christian, his life was changed. He learned to die to himself. Dr. Tauler became one of those who made the way ready for Luther, and the great Reformation he brought us. In this passage the Lord Jesus tells us how we can serve each other in this way.

What Is the Log?

What did the Lord Jesus say first? He said that it is possible for us to want to take out the tiny speck in another person's eye while there is a great big log of wood in our own eye! In that case, we simply cannot take the speck out of anyone else's eye. We cannot see properly ourselves. We are only pretending to help someone else if this is the case.

Now we all know what the Lord Jesus meant by the speck in some other person's eye. It is some fault which we think we can see in him. He may have done something to us which we did not like. He may have said something to us which was not good. But what did the Lord Jesus mean by the log in our own eye? May I suggest that it is our hard thoughts about the speck in someone else's eye? There is, no doubt, something wrong in the other person, but our hard thoughts about that wrong are also wrong! His fault has made us think harshly about him, or made us love him less. We have said bad things about him to others, or felt bitter about him. We do not want him to get on well. All of these things show a lack of love in *us*! And this, says the Lord Jesus, tells us that our lack of love is like a big log compared to our brother's tiny fault which is like a little speck of wood. He may not know it is there! Every time we point to someone and say "This is your fault," three fingers are pointing at us. But how often we have done it! While we have tried to deal with someone else's fault, God has seen this much bigger fault in our own hearts. May He have mercy upon us.

We do not need to think that the log is some very bad reaction on our part. The beginning of a hard thought is a log. The beginning of an unkind thought is a log. The first words we say about the faults of this person may be a log. It spoils our sight. We fail to see our brother as he really is. We forget that God still loves him. If we speak to our brother while we have these hard thoughts in our hearts, he will have hard thoughts about us. This is the law which rules our relationships with other people.

Take It to Calvary

"Take the log out of your own eye *first*," said the Lord Jesus. This is the first thing we must do. We must see that these hard thoughts toward our brother are sin. We must go with it in prayer to Calvary. We must see the Lord Jesus there and we must see again what He suffered for that sin. We must repent at His feet. We must be broken afresh, and confess our sin to Him. We must trust the Lord Jesus to make us clean in His precious blood. We must ask Him to fill us with His love for that person. If we believe His promise He will do this. Then we shall probably need to go to the other person. We must confess to him the sin that has been in our heart. We must tell him what the Lord Jesus has done for us, and ask him to forgive us too. Others may tell us that the sin we are confessing is not as bad as the other person's wrong. But we have been to Calvary. We are learning to live under the shadow of the Cross. We have seen our sin there. We can no longer compare our sin with that of another.

As we take these simple steps of repentance, the log in our eye will be taken away. We shall be able to see clearly how to take the speck out of the other person's eye. God will give us light about that person's need. We shall see things which neither he nor we had seen before. We may even find out that there is no speck there at all! We thought we could see one only because of the log in our own eye. On the other hand, we may see something in him which he himself hardly knew before—some hidden matter. Then, as God shows us the way, we must lovingly and humbly show this thing to him. He too will be able to see it, and go to the Cross and there confess his sin and have it put away. He will be glad to have our help to take the speck out. If he is a humble man, he will be grateful to us. He will know that we have not been helping him from wrong motives but because we love him and have a real concern for him.

When God tells us to bring something to a person's notice, let us not be afraid to do it. Let us not argue. Let us not keep on talking after we have said what the Lord told us to say. Let us just say it, and then stop. It is not our work to make the person "see" what we have told him. That is God's work. It takes time for a person to be willing to bend his stiff-necked self.

What should we do when someone brings something to our notice? Let us not try to defend ourselves. Let us not try to explain why we have done something. Let us listen quietly and thank the person who spoke to us. Then let us go to God and ask Him if the person was right. If the person was right, let us humbly go and tell him so. Then let us praise God together. There is no doubt that we need each other very much. We all have faults which we cannot see. These cannot be put right unless we are willing for God to use someone else to show them to us.

Chapter **8**

ARE YOU WILLING TO BE A SLAVE?_____

THE NEW TESTAMENT shows us clearly that the Lord Jesus wants us to take the low place of slaves. We have no choice in the matter. We cannot decide not to be slaves if we really want to be disciples of the Lord Jesus. Our new relationship with God depends on this very thing. We cannot know real fellowship with Christ and true holiness in our lives unless we are His slaves. We must, first of all, really understand what it means to be a slave. It is a humbling and self-emptying position. How can we ever be willing to take it? We must be ready to live, day by day, under the shadow of the Cross. We must always have in our minds the humbleness and the brokenness of the Lord Jesus.

Let us look at this subject and the effect it will have on each one of our lives. There are three things which must be said first. Only after we have understood these shall we be able to understand the low and humble place which the Lord Jesus wants us to take.

In the Old Testament two kinds of servants are mentioned. The first was the hired servant. He was an employee. He received wages. He had certain rights. The second kind was the bond servant or slave. He received no wages. He had no rights. He had no one to appeal to but his master. God told the people of Israel that they were not to make bond servants or slaves of their own people. They were allowed only to make people of other races their slaves.

But what do we find in the New Testament? What word is used there to describe the "servant of the Lord Jesus"? It is not the word for a hired servant; it is the word for a slave. What does this show us about our position? It shows us that we have no rights. We have no appeal except to our Master. We belong to Him; He can do with us as He wishes.

We must understand one more thing. We are the slaves of One who Himself was willing to become a slave! In this we see the wonderful humbleness of the Lord Jesus. "He always had the very nature of God, but he did not think that by force he should try to become equal with God. Instead, of his own free will he gave it all up, and took the nature of a servant"—*a slave!* See Philippians 2:6–7. And we are to be His slaves! He was willing to have no rights. He allowed Himself to be treated as God allowed men to treat Him. He did all this in order to serve men and bring them back to God. And He calls us—you and me—to be His slaves. He was always the humble One. He humbled Himself to serve the men and women His own hands had made. How low is our real place! This passage shows us something of what it means to be ruled by the Lord Jesus.

This shows us something else. As servants or slaves of the Lord Jesus we must also serve our fellow men and fellow women. "It is not ourselves that we preach; we preach Jesus Christ as Lord, and ourselves as your servants [slaves] for Jesus' sake" (2 Corinthians 4:5). The Lord Jesus judges the low place we take in relationship to Him by the low place we take in relationship to our brothers and sisters in Christ. If we are not willing to serve others in hard, humble ways, it shows that we are not really willing to serve Him. If we are not willing to serve Him, we cannot be in fellowship with Him!

Now let us apply all these things in a personal way to our own lives. Some time ago God spoke to me through the Lord's words in Luke 17:7–10:

"Suppose one of you has a servant who is plowing or looking after the sheep. When he comes in from the field, do you say to him, 'Hurry along and eat your meal'? Of course not! Instead, you say to him, 'Get my supper ready, then put on your apron and wait on me while I eat and drink; after that you may eat and drink.' The servant does not deserve thanks for obeying orders, does he? It is the same with you; when you have done all you have been told to do, say, 'We are ordinary servants; we have only done our duty.'"

Here we can see five marks of the slave. First of all, he must be willing to be given one job after another. He must not expect anyone to think about his wishes. Look at the servant in this parable. He had worked hard all day in the fields. When he came home, he had to cook his master's meal. Then he had to wait on him while he ate it. Not until he had done all this did he have anything to eat himself. The servant did not expect anything different. He just went and did as he was told. But we are often not willing to do this. When people expect us to do one job after another, we begin to complain. Bitter thoughts come into our hearts. But we must remember one thing. When we begin to complain we are acting as if we have some rights. But a slave has no rights.

Secondly, the servant must be willing to work hard and not be thanked for it. We often serve others, but at the same time have self-pity in our hearts. We complain bitterly if people take our service as if they had a right to it and do not thank us for it. But a slave must be willing for this. A hired servant may expect some wages, but not a bond servant.

Thirdly, after doing all this, the servant must not tell the other person that he is being selfish. As I read the passage, I felt that the master was somewhat selfish. He seems to have had little concern for his slave's welfare. But the slave did not tell him that. His work was to serve his master, whether he was selfish or not. That did not concern him. We may allow others to give us extra work to do. We may be willing not to be thanked for it. But in our hearts it is so easy to think that the other person is being selfish. But that is not the place of the slave. If others are selfish, the slave must serve them like his Master did. The slave will know in his own experience something of what the Lord felt when He became servant of all.

Fourthly, we must go one step further. After having done all these things, we cannot get proud and think that we are very good servants. We must confess that we are "ordinary" servants. In ourselves, we are of no use to God or men. We must confess again and again, like Paul did: "I know that good does not live in me—that is, in my human nature" (Romans 7:18). If we have acted like good slaves, we do not deserve thanks. Our hearts are naturally proud and unwilling to serve. If the Lord Jesus, who lives in us, has made us willing to serve others, we must give thanks to Him.

Fifthly, we come to the last step. We must not only do all that we have to do humbly and without complaining, but also we must admit that in all this we have done nothing more than our duty. In the beginning God made man to be His slave. When man refused to obey God, he sinned. When man is brought back to his proper place before God, he must again be His slave. It is not a special act of merit for a man to become a slave of God. This was the place for which God made him, and for which Christ has bought him.

So this is the Way of the Cross. It is the way that the Lord Jesus, God's humble bond servant, first walked for us. We are the bond servants of the Bond Servant. Should we not walk in the same way? It seems a hard road. We do not like to walk in it. It seems to go down and down. But yet it is the only road up. It was the way that the Lord Jesus reached the Throne of God. Do we want spiritual power and authority? Do we want our lives to bear fruit for God? Then we too must walk in this road. Those who walk in this road are happy people. The light can be seen in their faces. Their hearts overflow with the life of their Lord. What was true of the Lord is true of them: "Whoever humbles himself will be made great" (Luke 14:11). Before they were only humble sometimes. They did not really like being humble. But now humbleness is like the wife of their hearts. They are joined her forever. They live gladly with her day by day. If darkness and unrest come into their hearts, they know the reason. They know that at some point they have not been willing to walk humbly in the paths of meekness and brokenness. But as soon as they turn from this sin, humbleness is always ready to welcome them back to walk with her again.

This brings us to the most important matter of repentance. How can we enter into a more abundant life? We cannot do it by making up our minds that we shall be more humble in the future. First of all we must really repent for the wrong things we have done and are still doing. Perhaps we are not willing to ask some person's forgiveness for some wrong we have done to him. The Lord Jesus did not take on Himself the nature of a slave only to show us how to live. No, He became Man to die for our sins on the cross. By shedding His precious blood on the cross He prepared the fountain in which our sins can be washed away. How can the value of this blood be applied to our sins? It will not happen while we are proud and unbroken. First of all, we must repent because of what we are and what we have done. We must allow God's light to come into every part of our hearts. It must shine on each one of our relationships. God will show us our sins of pride. We shall see that it was because of these that the Lord Jesus had to come from heaven and die on the cross. This was the only way in which they could be forgiven. We must confess these sins to Him and claim His forgiveness. We must ask others to forgive us too. This will make us humble. We shall have to crawl through the door of the broken ones. But on the other side of the door, we shall come into light and glory. We shall be walking on the Highway of Holiness and Humbleness.

Chapter 9

THE POWER OF THE BLOOD OF THE LAMB

IN THESE DAYS many of us are beginning to understand the message of revival. It is making us think about ourselves. It is a very simple message, but it is one which throws light on our whole being. What is this message? It is this: There is only one thing in all the world which can hinder a Christian from experiencing victory and fellowship with God. There is only one thing which can stop a Christian from being filled with the Holy Spirit. That thing is sin. Sin has many forms, and any one of these can be the hindrance. But there is also only one thing which can make us clean from sin. It is this: the power of the blood of the Lord Jesus. What gives the blood of the Lord Jesus its mighty power with God to make men free from sin? We must understand this in order to understand how we can experience its full power in our own lives.

The Bible shows us what the Lord Jesus did for us when He shed His blood on the cross. It tells us of

the many blessings which we receive through His
blood. "Christ's death on the cross has made peace
with God for all by his blood" (Colossians 1:20, *The
Living Bible*). "[Christ] bought our freedom with his
blood and forgave us all our sins" (Colossians 1:14,
The Living Bible). The Lord Jesus Himself said, "Whoever ... drinks my blood has eternal life" (John 6:54).
"Our brothers won the victory over [Satan] by the
blood of the Lamb" (Revelation 12:11). "The blood
of Jesus, his Son, makes us clean from all our sins"
(1 John 1:7). "His blood will make our consciences
clean from useless works, so that we may serve the
living God" (Hebrews 9:14). "We may walk right into
the very Holy of Holies where God is, because of
the blood of Jesus" (Hebrews 10:19, *The Living Bible*).
How did this come about? How did the blood of
Christ get this wonderful power?

With this question we must link a second one.
How can we experience the full power of the blood
of Jesus in our own lives? Too often there is sin, unrest, and lack of power in our lives. We do not enjoy
the fellowship of God's presence all the day. Why is
this? Why do we not fully experience the power of
the blood to make us clean, give us peace, and fill us
with life and power?

Where Does the Power of the Blood Come From?

Let us look at the book of Revelation. In this book
the blood of Christ is described as the "blood of the
Lamb" (Revelation 7:14). These words give us part
of the answer to our question. It was not the blood

of the Lion or the Fighter, but the blood of the *Lamb*. The power of the blood comes from the lamb-like nature of the *One* who shed it. That is why it is so powerful with God for men. It was in His death that the Lord Jesus showed most completely His lamb-like nature.

Why is the Lord Jesus described as the Lamb? First of all, it is a description of His work. He came to be the Sacrifice for our sin. What did an Israelite do when he knew he had sinned and needed to get right with God? He would bring a lamb (or a goat) as a sacrifice. The animal would be killed and its blood sprinkled on the altar. The Lord Jesus, the Son of God, was the One who showed the true meaning of all the lambs which men had sacrificed. "Here is the Lamb of God who takes away the sin of the world" (John 1:29).

But the name "the Lamb" has a deeper meaning as well. It shows us His nature. Like a lamb, He is gentle and humble in spirit (Matthew 11:29). He did not take revenge. He Himself said: "I have come down from heaven to do the will of him who sent me, *not my own will*" (John 6:38). He came so that men might be blessed and saved. If His nature had not been that of the Lamb, He would have had hard thoughts when men treated Him badly. But "He was humble and walked the path of obedience to death— his death on the cross" (Philippians 2:8). He loved His Father and He loved us, and so endured it all to save us. Men did what they wished to Him. For our sakes He gave Himself into their hands. "When he was insulted, he did not answer back with an insult; when he suffered, he did not threaten" (1 Peter 2:23). He did not claim His rights. He did not hit back. He had no hard thoughts. He did not complain. He was very different from what we are! When He knew that it was God's plan that wicked men should put Him on the cross, He bowed His head to death. He was put to death like a lamb. Isaiah prophesied about Him as the Lamb: "He was brought as a lamb to the slaughter; and as a sheep before her shearers is dumb, so he stood silent before the ones condemning him" (Isaiah 53:7). Men flogged Him with a whip. They laughed at Him. They spit on Him. They pulled the hair from His beard. They laid the cross on His back and made Him carry it to Calvary. There they nailed Him to the cross. He was lifted up to die. After He died a soldier pierced His side with a spear, and His blood flowed out. All these things happened because the Lord Jesus was the Lamb. He did all this to pay the price of my sin. It is true that He was the Lamb because He died on the cross, but it is also true that He died on the cross because He was the Lamb.

Let us always remember this fact about the blood. The blood shows us the humbleness and self-sacrifice of the Lamb. This is what gives the blood its wonderful power with God. Look at Hebrews 9:14. There the writer links together the blood of Christ and His offering Himself as a sacrifice to God. "How much more is accomplished by the blood of Christ! Through the eternal Spirit he offered himself as a perfect sacrifice to God." This is why the blood has such power with God. He places great value on that which is offered to Him. He wants to see in men the nature of the Lamb. He wants men who will humbly obey Him. He wants men who will give up their wills to do His will. That was why God made man in the first place. Man sinned when he refused to walk in the path of obedience to God. This has been the real heart of sin ever since. The Lord Jesus came to earth as a Man to live in obedience to God. When the Father saw His Son always obeying Him He said: "This is my own dear Son, with whom I am well pleased" (Matthew 3:17). In obedience to the will of the Father, He shed His blood on the cross. This is why His blood is so precious to God. This is why His blood can wash away all the sins of men.

How Can We Experience This Power in Our Own Lives?

This is our second question. Our own hearts can tell us the answer. We must look on the Lamb, who bowed His head for us on the cross. We must be willing to let the nature which ruled Him rule us. We must bend our necks in brokenness as He bent His. It is the nature of the Lamb—as we have seen—that gives to the blood its power. As we are willing to be partakers in the nature of the Lamb so shall we know its full power in our lives. He died so that we can be partakers of His nature (Philippians 2:5 and 1 Corinthians 2:16). In Galatians 5:22–23 we read of the fruit of the Holy Spirit: love, joy, peace, patience, kind-

ness, goodness, faithfulness, humility, and self-control. These all show us the lamb-like nature of the
Lord Jesus. These are the things with which the Holy
Spirit wants to fill us. The Lord Jesus is now sitting
in glory on the throne of God, but He is still the Lamb.
(The book of Revelation tells us this.) He wants us to
share His nature and be like Him.

Are We Ready to Do This?

This is a most important question. In each one of
us is a hard self which does not want to bow its head
to God. It seeks its own rights. It does not like others
to tell it what to do. If we want to have the nature of
the Lamb, that hard self must be broken. Only in this
way shall we really experience the cleansing power
of the blood. It is not enough just to pray to be made
clean. It is not enough to pray that peace may come
back to our hearts. No, we must be willing to be broken about each sin which is hindering us. We must
partake of the humbleness of the Lamb about this
matter. Until we do this we shall not be made clean
from that sin. How does sin come about? It is always
from our hard, unbroken self. It likes to be proud.
To find peace through the blood we must go to the
root of each sin. We must definitely turn away from
it in repentance. This will always make us humble.

We should not *try* to be humble like the Lord Jesus.
All we must do is walk in the light. We must ask
God to show us any sins which may be in our lives.
He will show them to us. We must turn from them
and give up our wills to Him. It will not be easy. We

may think these things very small and not worth writing about. Our pride will be hurt as we put them right. We may have to confess to someone something we have done, and ask his forgiveness. We may have to give back something which we have taken wrongly. We may have to do something which we refused to do before. We must give up any rights we thought we had. (The Lord Jesus had no rights. How can we claim any?) He may show us that we must go to someone who has done us a wrong and confess that our hard thoughts about him have been the greater wrong. (The Lord Jesus did not have hard thoughts about anyone. Have we any right to?) He may want us to be open with our friends so that they will know what we are really like. This is the only way they can have real fellowship with us.

It will make us humble to have to do this. We shall have to turn completely from our pride and selfishness but this will help us to be really broken. In this way we shall become humble partakers of the nature of the Lamb. We must be willing for this in each matter in our lives, and then the blood of the Lamb will be able to make us clean from all sin. We shall walk with God and be clothed in white. We shall experience His peace in our hearts.

Chapter **10**

DO WE SAY THAT WE ARE NOT LIKE EVERYBODY ELSE?—

WE PROBABLY know the story which the Lord Jesus told about the Pharisee and the Tax Collector (Publican). It is found in Luke 18:9–14. The Pharisee was sure of his own goodness and despised everybody else. We like to think how wrong he was in this. But we forget that the Pharisee is supposed to be a picture of us! If we do this, it just shows us how like him we really are. A Sunday school teacher once told the children in the class this parable. She finished her lesson with the words: "Now, children, we can thank God that we are not like this Pharisee!" She did not realize that in saying this she was showing just how much like a Pharisee she really was. We can very easily be like this when God is wanting to humble us at the Cross of Jesus. We like to say we are not like everybody else when God wants to show us the sins in our hearts which are stopping our own lives from being revived.

God's Picture of Man's Heart

What was wrong about the way the Pharisee thought? What is wrong about the way we think? We shall not really understand this until we see what God says about man's heart. The Lord Jesus Himself said: "From the inside, from a man's heart, come the evil ideas which lead him to do immoral things, to rob, kill, commit adultery, be greedy, and do all sorts of evil things; deceit, indecency, jealousy, slander, pride, and folly—all these evil things come from inside a man and make him unclean" (Mark 7:21–23). Paul gives the same dark picture of man's heart in his letter to the Galatians: "What human nature does is quite plain. It shows itself in immoral, filthy, and indecent actions; in worship of idols and witchcraft. People become enemies, they fight, become jealous, angry, and ambitious. They separate into parties and groups; they are envious, get drunk, have orgies, and do other things like these" (Galatians 5:19–21). What a picture! Jeremiah says the same: "The heart is the most deceitful thing there is, and desperately wicked. No one can really know how bad it is!" This is God's picture of the human heart.

This is what fallen human nature—the old self—is really like. And it is exactly the same in the unbeliever as in the most keen Christian! Can this kind of thing come out of the hearts of Christian preachers, evangelists, and missionaries? Yes indeed! There is only one thing about the Christian which is really beautiful, and that is Jesus Christ Himself! God wants us to see that this is true in our experience. He wants us to be broken to see that our self can do *nothing* to help us. He wants us to let the Lord Jesus show His goodness and holiness in us. He must do everything! This is the only way we shall get the victory.

Do We Make a Liar out of God?

We have seen how God describes man's heart. Now we can see what the Pharisee did. He said: "I thank you, God, that I am not greedy, dishonest, or immoral, like everybody else." In other words, he said that what God says is true of every man's heart was not true of his heart. His meaning was this: "These things are without doubt true of other men. They are true of this taxgatherer: that is why he is now confessing them. But, God, they are not true of me!" In saying this, he was making a liar out of God! John says this plainly: "If we say that we have not sinned, we make a liar out of God" (1 John 1:10). The reason is that God says we have sinned! But I am sure that this man really thought that what he said was true. He really did believe that these things were *not* true of himself. In fact, he thought that God had given him his goodness, and he thanked Him for it. He did not see that what he had said was against God's word. He did not see that what God said about all men was true of him as well.

The tax collector, however, beat upon his breast and confessed to God that he was a sinner. Does this mean that he was really a worse sinner than the Pharisee? Not at all. The tax collector had seen that

what God says about man's heart was, to his great
sorrow, true of his own heart; but the Pharisee had
not. The Pharisee thought that it was enough not to
do some outward sins. He had not yet understood
that God does not look on the outward appearance,
but on the heart (1 Samuel 16:7). In God's sight the
man who looks at a woman and wants to possess
her is guilty of committing adultery with her in his
heart (Matthew 5:27). In the same way, the man who
hates his brother is a murderer in God's sight (1 John
3:15). Envy is as bad as actual stealing. To rule
harshly and wrongly in the home is as bad as unfair
dealing in the market.

How often have we been like the Pharisee! Many
times God has shown others their sins, and has
wanted to show us our sins as well. We have said:
"These things may be true of others, but they are
not true of me." Perhaps we really thought that what
we said was true. We have heard of others who have
humbled themselves. We have heard about the
things which they had to confess. We have heard
some of the bad things which they have had to put
right. Perhaps we have despised them for some of
these things. Perhaps we have been really glad that
they have been blessed. But we do not feel that we
have anything in our lives which we need to be broken about. Is that true of us? Then, my beloved brothers and sisters, we can be sure that it is not because
these things are not there. They are, but we have not
yet seen them. We have had wrong ideas about ourselves. What God says about us must be true. In one

form or another He can see all these things in us. We
need to see them for ourselves, and then take them
to the Cross and allow God to deal with them.

What are some of these things God sees? Are we
really being selfish, although we may not realize it?
Are we proud? Do we like to tell ourselves how good
we are? Are we jealous and have hard thoughts of
others? Are we impatient? Do we try to hide our real
selves? Are we fearful and shy? Are we always hon-
est? Do we try to trick others? Do we have unclean
thoughts? Are we guilty of sexual sins, in thought if
not in action? Are *any* of these things true of us? If
so, we ourselves may be blind to it. Perhaps some
other person has done a wrong to us. We think about
this. We are not willing to accept this wrong. We are
not being meek and humble like our Lord Jesus. We
can see that this other man wants *his* rights and *his*
way; we do not see that what we want is *our* rights
and *our* way just as much. Yet we know that there is
something missing from our lives. We are not enjoying a living fellowship with God. His power is
not seen in our service. Even sin which we are not
aware of is still sin with God. It separates us from
Him. This sin may be only a small thing. But if we
ask Him, God will readily show it to us.

When we do not recognize that what God says
about man's heart is true, we can easily fall into another error. Not only do we say that there is nothing
really wrong with us, but also that there is nothing
really wrong with our own loved ones. We do not
like it when they see their own sins. We do not want

to see them being humbled. We hasten to say it is not really their fault. We do not want them to confess their sin. We do not see the real truth about ourselves; we do not see the real truth about our loved ones—and we do not want to! But if we do this, we are trying to say that what God says about them is not true. We are making out that God is telling lies about them, just as we do about ourselves. And just as this stops us from experiencing God's blessing, so it stops them from experiencing it too.

We need a deep hunger for real fellowship with God. Only this will make us cry to God to show us the real truth about ourselves. When He does so, we must do what He tells us to do.

Confessing That God Is Right

This brings us to the tax collector. We have seen what God says about man's heart. When the tax collector confessed his sin, he simply admitted that what God said about him was true. Before, he may have been like the Pharisee. He may not have believed that what God said about him was really true. But the Holy Spirit had shown him things in his life which showed that God was right. He was broken before God. He admitted that all God had said about him was right. He also confessed that God was right in punishing him for his sin. His prayer was like that of Nehemiah years before: "Every time you punished us you were being perfectly fair; we have sinned so greatly that you gave us only what we deserved" (Nehemiah 9:33).

This is what true confession of sin will do. We shall be really broken. We shall confess that our sin was not just a little mistake. We shall confess that it is something which comes from our real nature. We shall not say: "It is not really like I am. I do not usually have such thoughts or do such things." We shall see that our sin shows us what we are really like. Our sin shows us what proud, bad, unclean things we are. It shows that what God says about us is true. It really is like me to have such thoughts and do such things. David came to know this. Listen to his prayer: "It is against you and you alone I sinned, and did this terrible thing. You saw it all, and your sentence against me is just" (Psalm 51:4). When God tells us that we must make such a confession, let us not be afraid to do it. It will not bring shame to the Name of the Lord Jesus. It will do just the opposite. Such confessions bring glory to God. We are admitting that we know that He is right. This confession also brings us to a new experience of victory in Christ. It again declares what Paul declared: "I know that good does not live in me—that is, in my human nature" (Romans 7:18). This will make us stop trying to make our incurable human natures holy. Instead we shall take the Lord Jesus as our holiness, and take His life as our life.

Peace and Cleansing

But the tax collector did more than admit that God was right in what He said about him. He pointed to the sacrifice on the altar. As he did this, the tax collector found cleansing and peace with God. What was the real meaning of his words, "O God, have pity on me, a sinner"? The words "have pity" mean "be propitiated." What does this mean? The Jews knew that their sacrifices were to propitiate God, i.e., they were offered to take away their sins. The only way to propitiate God was by offering a sacrifice. It is very likely that at the time the tax collector said these words, the lamb for the daily burnt offering was being offered on the altar in the temple.

It is the same with us. When a man comes to see that what God says about him is true, he will be broken before God. Then God will show to him the Lamb of God on the cross of Calvary. The man will see that the Lord Jesus shed His blood to put away his sins. God tells us in His Word that we are sinners; He has also made the way for us to be made clean from our sins. The Lamb was killed so that our names might be written in the book of life before the world began (Revelation 13:8). He humbly bore my sins. They have been taken away. I must now, in true brokenness, confess my sins to Him. I must put my faith in His blood. Then He will make me clean from all my sins. I shall enjoy peace with God in my heart. Once again I shall experience fellowship with God. I shall walk with Him clothed in white.

In this simple way we must be willing to confess that God is right in what He says about us. We must see that the blood of the Lord Jesus makes us clean from all sin. This makes it possible for us to live more closely with the Lord Jesus than was ever possible before. We shall be able at all times to live with Him in the Most Holy Place. We must walk with Him in the light. As we do this, He will show us at all times the beginnings of sin. If we let these grow, they will stop His life from flowing through us. These things come from our old, proud nature. All God can do is to judge that nature. We must never say that what God says of us is not true. We must always be willing to admit that He is right, and to say, "You are right, Lord. That is just what I am." When God shows us any sin in us, we must be willing to confess it to Him. He will make us clean from it. As we do this, His blood will continuously make us free from all sin. His life will be continuously flowing into us, for the things which hinder will be stopped at the beginning. The Lord Jesus will be continuously filling us with His Spirit. This means that we must have humble, repentant hearts (Isaiah 57:15). We must be willing for God to show us the smallest things in our lives which do not please Him. If we do this, we shall dwell in the high and holy place with Him. We shall experience continuous revival.

Here, then, is the choice we must make. We can be like the Pharisee. We can be sure of our own goodness. We can thank God that we are not like everybody else. We can go home without getting a blessing. Our souls will be dry. We shall not be in fellowship with God. Or we can be like the tax collector. We can admit to God that what He says about us is true. If we do this, we shall enter into peace, fellowship, and victory through the blood of Jesus.